KU-390-905

I2747504

nickelodeon

TEENAGE MUTANT NINJA TURTLES™

AMAZING ADVENTURES

Tea-Time For A Turtle
Story by **Peter DiCicco**
Art by **Chad Thomas**

Quiet Please
Story by **Ian Flynn**
Art by **Coleman Engle**

The Tournament
Story by **Fabian Rangel**
Art by **Billy Martin**

Special thanks to Joan Hilty & Linda Lee
for their invaluable assistance.

ISBN: 978-1-63140-886-1

nickelodeon

For international rights, contact **licensing@idwpublishing.com**

20 19 18 17 1 2 3 4

IDW
www.IDWPUBLISHING.com

Ted Adams, CEO & Publisher • **Greg Goldstein**, President & COO • **Robbie Robbins**, EVP/Sr. Graphic Artist • **Chris Ryall**, Chief Creative Officer • **David Hedgecock**, Editor-in-Chief • **Laurie Windrow**, Senior Vice President of Sales & Marketing • **Matthew Ruzicka**, CPA, Chief Financial Officer • **Lorelei Bunjes**, VP of Digital Services • **Jerry Bennington**, VP of New Product Development

Facebook: **facebook.com/idwpublishing** • Twitter: **@idwpublishing** • YouTube: **youtube.com/idwpublishing**
Tumblr: **tumblr.idwpublishing.com** • Instagram: **instagram.com/idwpublishing**

Originally published as TEENAGE MUTANT NINJA TURTLES: AMAZING ADVENTURES issues #5–8.

Job Security
Story by **Ian Flynn**
Art by **Chad Thomas**

You Win Some, You Shoe Some!
Story by **Caleb Goellner**
Art by **Dave Alvarez**

Cowa-Booyakasha
Story by **Ian Flynn**
Art by **Jon Sommariva**
Colors by **John Rauch**

Colors by **Heather Breckel**
Letters and Collection Design by **Shawn Lee**
Series Edits by **Bobby Curnow**

Cover by **Jon Sommariva**
Collection Edits by **Justin Eisinger** and **Alonzo Simon**
Publisher: **Ted Adams**

Art by **Jon Sommariva**

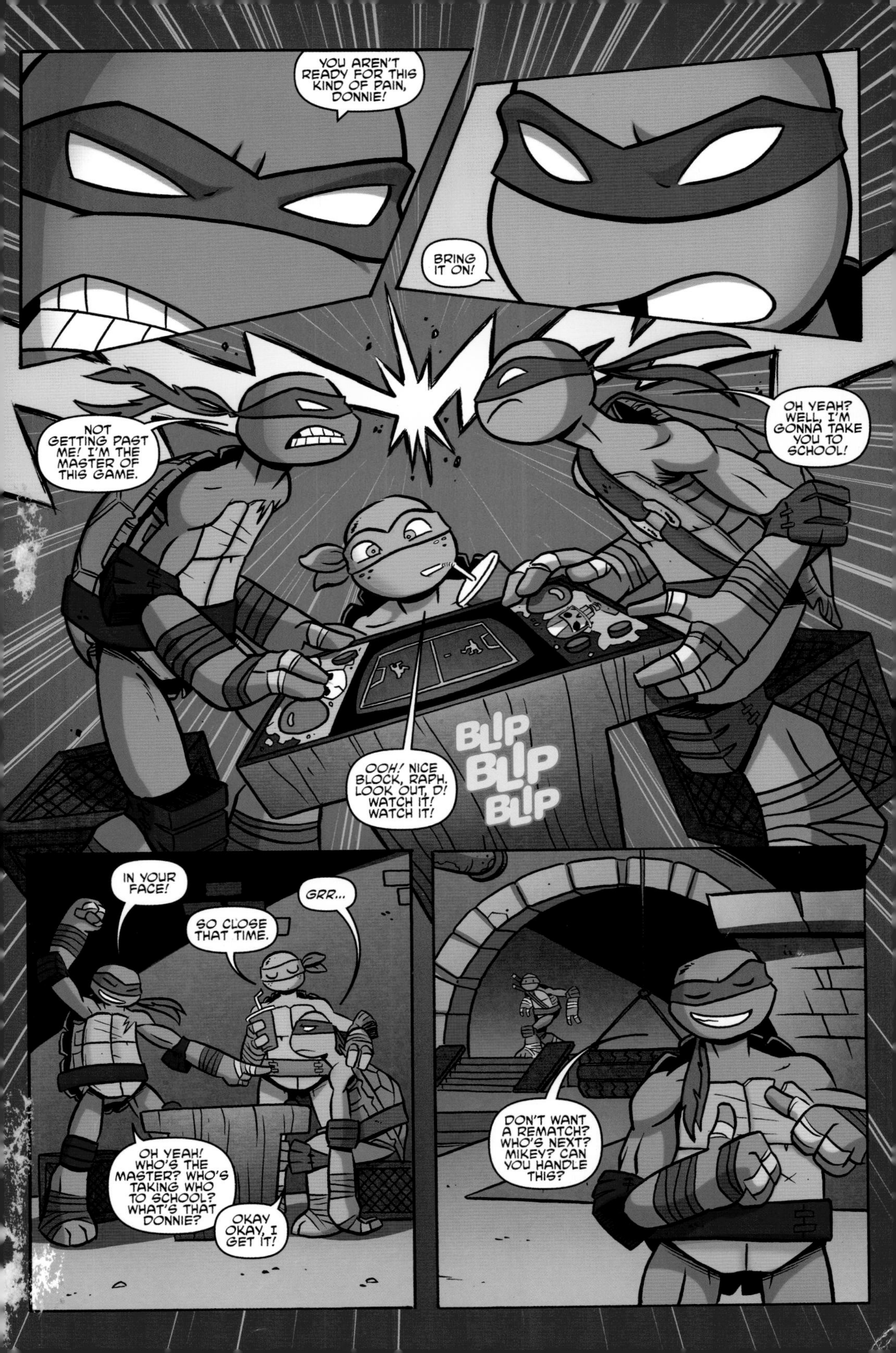
YOU AREN'T READY FOR THIS KIND OF PAIN, DONNIE!
BRING IT ON!
NOT GETTING PAST ME! I'M THE MASTER OF THIS GAME.
OH YEAH? WELL, I'M GONNA TAKE YOU TO SCHOOL!
OOH! NICE BLOCK, RAPH. LOOK OUT, D! WATCH IT! WATCH IT!
BLIP BLIP BLIP
IN YOUR FACE!
SO CLOSE THAT TIME.
GRR...
OH YEAH! WHO'S THE MASTER? WHO'S TAKING WHO TO SCHOOL? WHAT'S THAT DONNIE?
OKAY OKAY, I GET IT!
DON'T WANT A REMATCH? WHO'S NEXT? MIKEY? CAN YOU HANDLE THIS?

LEO? UP FOR A LITTLE FRIENDLY COMPETITION?
YEAH, REAL FRIENDLY.

HEY, I CAN'T PLAY WITH AMATEURS ALL DAY. WHAT DO YOU SAY, LEO?
OH... *UH*... NOT THIS TIME. I GOTTA... *UM*... GO OUT FOR SOME CITY STEALTH TRAINING.

COME ON, MAN. NOT ANOTHER LATE-NIGHT NINJA RETREAT.
WE ALREADY SPEND ENOUGH TIME FIGHTING SHREDDER AND EVERY CRAZY MUTANT THAT POPS UP AS IT IS.
YOU NEED TO LEARN TO CUT LOOSE, MAN. TAKE A NIGHT OFF.
THAT'S WHAT I'M DOING.
I'LL GIVE YOU A LITTLE COMPETITION, DON.
OH, YOU'RE ON!
BY TRAINING?
YEAH... I CUT LOOSE EVERY NIGHT... BY TRAINING... *HEH*.
EH, SUIT YOURSELF.
HE'S CRAZY.
YOU KNOW LEO. HE ALWAYS PUSHES HIMSELF TO TRAIN HARDER THAN ANY OF US.
YEAH, AND MAYBE HE'S ON SOME MISSION...

"...GATHERING INFO ON SHREDDER..."
"...PREPARING TO TAKE HIM DOWN ONCE AND FOR ALL!"
MORE TEA, MISTER TURTLE?
THANK YOU, CHLOE. DON'T MIND IF I DO.
TEA-TIME FOR A TURTLE

VERY GOOD. PINKIES UP, AND SIP.
MMM... EXCELLENT TEA, CHLOE.
WHY, THANK YOU, MISTER TURTLE.

WHAT'S THAT?
OH, TEDDY IS ENJOYING IT TOO.
WELL, OF COURSE HE DOES, SILLY. IT'S HIS FAVORITE.

WELL, THAT MAKES TEDDY AT LEAST MORE CIVILIZED THAN RAPH.

OOH! IS THAT THE OTHER TURTLE LIKE YOU? CAN I MEET HIM?
UM... WELL, MY BROTHERS DON'T REALLY LIKE--
BROTHERS? YOU DIDN'T TELL ME YOU HAD MORE THAN ONE!

PLEASE, CAN I MEET THEM?
PLEEAAAASSSE!
I DON'T KNOW... THEY'RE NOT REALLY TEA-TIME KIND OF GUYS.

BACK IN THE LAIR...
YEP, STILL REIGNING CHAMPION. YOU NEED MORE PRACTICE, MIKEY!
FACE IT, YOU'RE WORSE THAN DONNIE. EVEN WORSE THAN ICE CREAM KITTY. SHE COULD MOP THE FLOOR WITH YOU!
OH YEAH? MOP THE FLOOR WITH THIS!
FLORP
HAHAHA! WHATSAMATTER, RAPH? CAN'T HANDLE A LITTLE FRIENDLY COMPETITION?
WHY I OUGHTA--!
WAIT! LET'S TALK ABOUT THIS...
AAAHHH! RAPH!
CRASH
WHOA! WAIT A MINUTE--! ACK!
WHACK
SLAM
BONK
YOU PROMISED NO MORE SHELL WEDGIES!
OH, I'LL GIVE YOU A SHELL WEDGIE!
AAH! GET OFF!
BUZZ
GUYS! KNOCK IT OFF! IT'S APRIL.

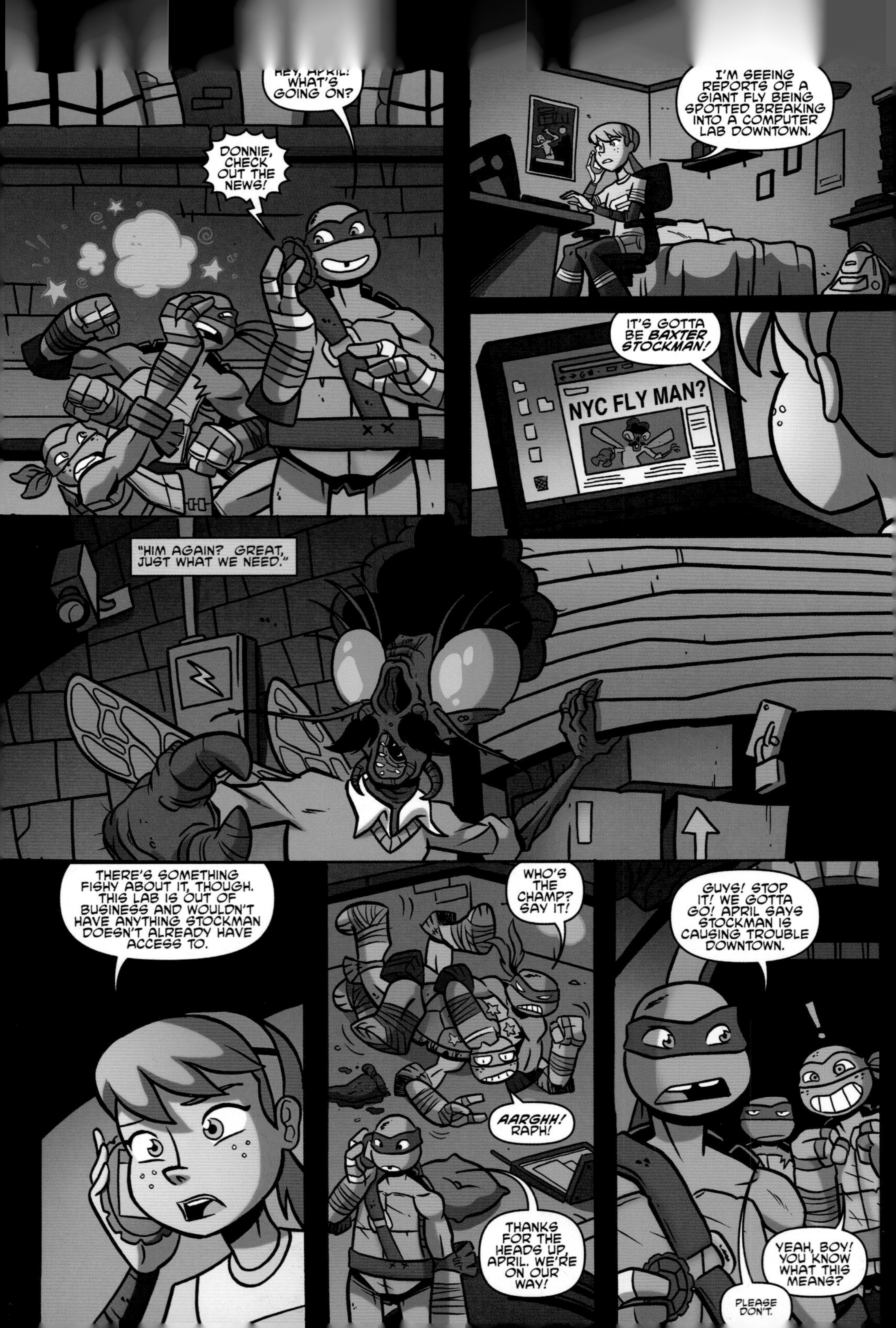

HEY, APRIL! WHAT'S GOING ON?
DONNIE, CHECK OUT THE NEWS!
I'M SEEING REPORTS OF A GIANT FLY BEING SPOTTED BREAKING INTO A COMPUTER LAB DOWNTOWN.
IT'S GOTTA BE BAXTER STOCKMAN!
NYC FLY MAN?
"HIM AGAIN? GREAT, JUST WHAT WE NEED."
THERE'S SOMETHING FISHY ABOUT IT, THOUGH. THIS LAB IS OUT OF BUSINESS AND WOULDN'T HAVE ANYTHING STOCKMAN DOESN'T ALREADY HAVE ACCESS TO.
WHO'S THE CHAMP? SAY IT!
AARGHH! RAPH!
THANKS FOR THE HEADS UP, APRIL. WE'RE ON OUR WAY!
GUYS! STOP IT! WE GOTTA GO! APRIL SAYS STOCKMAN IS CAUSING TROUBLE DOWNTOWN.
!
YEAH, BOY! YOU KNOW WHAT THIS MEANS?
PLEASE DON'T.

TUR-FLY-TLE! **BUZZ BUZZ!**
ENOUGH WITH THE TURFLYTLE! LET'S JUST TAKE CARE OF THAT BUG.
AW...
UM, DO YOU THINK SENSEI WILL BE MAD IF WE DON'T CLEAN UP BEFORE WE GO?
HMMM...
NOPE!
LET'S GO!
I'LL CALL LEO ON THE WAY.
WHAT IS THE COMMOTION GOING ON– BOYS?
BOYS?
SIIIIIIIIIIGH

MISTER TURTLE!
BUZZ
OOPS! WAS THAT ME? SORRY... HEH-HEH...
WHAT DID WE SAY ABOUT PHONES DURING TEA TIME?
I KNOW BUT I SHOULD PROBABLY—
NO PHONES AT THE TABLE. THAT'S THE RULE!
I KNOW RULES ARE RULES AND EVERYTHING, BUT IT MIGHT BE IMPORTANT.
MORE IMPORTANT THAN TEA-TIME?
NO LUCK WITH LEO YET.
EH, IT'S JUST BAXTER. HE'S LIKE A LEVEL ONE BOSS.
YEAH, EVEN YOU TWO CAN TAKE THAT GUY.
YEAH— HEY!

YOU KNOW, CHLOE, IT IS GETTING KIND OF LATE.
MY BROTHERS ARE GONNA BE WORRIED ABOUT ME.
YOUR BROTHERS?
OOH! DO I FINALLY GET TO MEET THEM?
UM... ER... I DON'T THINK IT'S A GOOD IDEA.
IF I DON'T GET TO MEET YOUR BROTHERS, YOU HAVE TO STAY FOR ONE MORE CUP OF TEA.
MY DADDY IS STILL IN THE NEXT ROOM AND HE HASN'T COME TO TUCK ME IN YET.
THUMP
OKAY OKAY, YOU WIN... ONE MORE CUP OF TEA.
AND THEN IT'S YOUR BEDTIME.
"I'M SURE THE GUYS WILL CALL AGAIN IF THEY REALLY NEED ME."

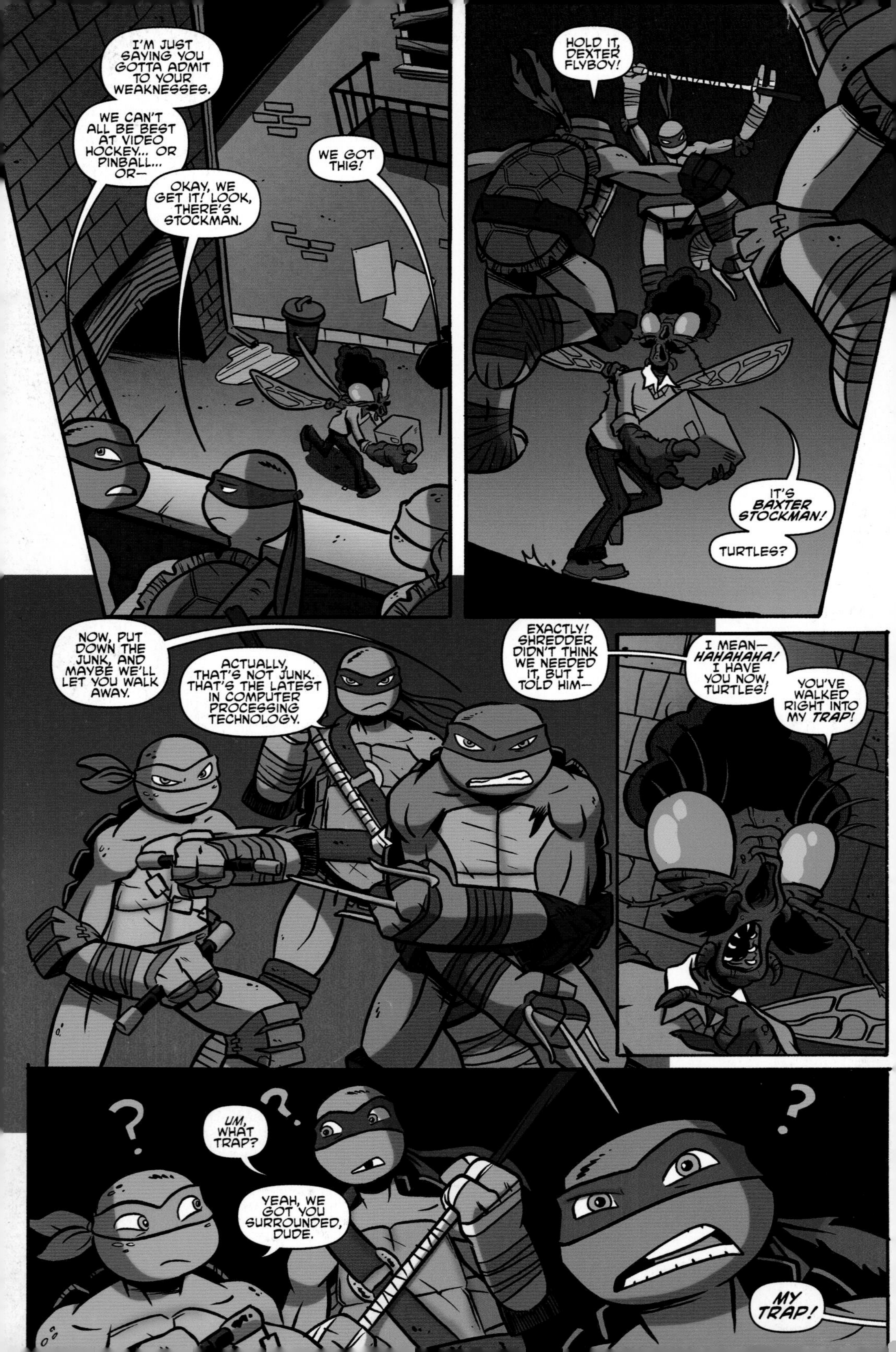
I'M JUST SAYING YOU GOTTA ADMIT TO YOUR WEAKNESSES.
WE CAN'T ALL BE BEST AT VIDEO HOCKEY... OR PINBALL... OR—
OKAY, WE GET IT! LOOK, THERE'S STOCKMAN.
WE GOT THIS!
HOLD IT, DEXTER FLYBOY!
IT'S BAXTER STOCKMAN!
TURTLES?
NOW, PUT DOWN THE JUNK, AND MAYBE WE'LL LET YOU WALK AWAY.
ACTUALLY, THAT'S NOT JUNK. THAT'S THE LATEST IN COMPUTER PROCESSING TECHNOLOGY.
EXACTLY! SHREDDER DIDN'T THINK WE NEEDED IT, BUT I TOLD HIM—
I MEAN— HAHAHAHA! I HAVE YOU NOW, TURTLES!
YOU'VE WALKED RIGHT INTO MY TRAP!
?
UM, WHAT TRAP?
?
YEAH, WE GOT YOU SURROUNDED, DUDE.
?
MY TRAP!

NOWHERE TO RUN, REPTILES!
OKAY, MAYBE WE DON'T GOT THIS!
WATCH OUT!
DON'T QUIT ON ME NOW—WHOA!
AHH! NEVER MIND. TRY LEO AGAIN!
HURRY, DUDE!
YOU CANNOT ESCAPE ME!
LEO'S NOT PICKING UP! WHAT ARE WE GONNA DO?!
TAKE THAT, BUG BOY!

AAAAHHHHH!
BUZZ

LAST TIME...
LEO SNUCK OUT FOR "SPECIAL TRAINING" WHICH WAS ACTUALLY TEA-TIME WITH CHLOE, A LITTLE GIRL WITH A BIG IMAGINATION.
WHILE THE OTHER TURTLES WERE GETTING INTO THE SPIRIT OF COMPETITION...
BUT THEN THEY CONFRONTED BAXTER STOCKMAN ON THEIR OWN...
AND WALKED INTO A TRAP
AAAAAHHHH!
LEO, WHERE ARE YOU?!

UGH!
BANK
HERE COMES WAVE TWO, BROS!
RAPH!
GAME OVER, TURTLES!
FEEL THE STING OF TURFLYTLE! BUZZ BUZZ!
NOT YET, KITTY CAT!
HEY— GAH!
NO! YOU IDIOT!
COWABUNGA!
THAT'S ONE FOR MIKEY!
DOES THAT CAT EVER RUN OUT OF AMMO?
GET LEO DOWN HERE! HURRY!
I'VE BEEN TRYING! THIS ISN'T LIKE HIM. WHAT IF HE'S IN WORSE TROUBLE?

MEANWHILE...
OH NO!
BUZZ
MISTER TURTLE, YOU PROMISED!
I KNOW, I'M SORRY, BUT THE GUYS WOULDN'T KEEP CALLING IF IT WASN'T AN EMERGENCY.
BUZZ
DONNIE! WHAT'S GOING ON? WHERE ARE YOU GUYS?
LEO, THANK GOODNESS! TIGER CLAW SET A TRAP FOR US!
PINGING YOU OUR LOCATION. HURRY! HE'S A FAST CAT!
I'M BLOCKS AWAY. I'LL BE RIGHT THERE!

SORRY, CHLOE, I HAVE TO RUN! ACK—!
NO! IF YOU'RE GOING, I WANT TO GO WITH YOU. YOU PROMISED!
I KNOW, BUT THE GUYS ARE IN DANGER AND NEED MY HELP. IT'S TOO DANGEROUS FOR YOU TO COME WITH ME.
BESIDES, LOOK! IT'S PAST YOUR BEDTIME. YOU SHOULD BE GETTING TO SLEEP.
OKAY, MISTER TURTLE. BUT ONLY IF YOU PROMISE TO COME BACK TOMORROW.
I PROMISE, BUT ONLY IF YOU PROMISE TO STAY HERE AND GO TO SLEEP.
I PROMISE...

MOMENTS LATER, BLOCKS AWAY...
LEO TAKES A SHORT CUT AND...
GIVE UP, TURTLES! YOU CAN'T RUN FOREVER!
BZZZ! YES! YOU CANNOT ESCAPE US, FOOLS!
HEY SPECKMAN!
IT'S STOCK—HEY! WHERE'D YOU COME FROM?!
HA! WITH THAT MANY EYES, YOU SHOULD PAY ATTENTION TO YOUR SURROUNDINGS!
I HAVE YOU IN MY SIGHTS, REPTILE! LET'S SEE IF YOUR COLD BLOOD CAN HANDLE A DEEP FREEZE!
STOCKMAN, YOU FOOL!
BLAM!
CLINK

LEO!
YOU MADE IT!
WHAT TOOK YOU SO LONG?!
KIND OF A LONG STORY...
I DON'T THINK I HAVE TIME TO TELL IT.
GRRR... NO MATTER. I'LL LET THE FLY THAW OUT LATER.
MOTEL
I LIKE THESE ODDS, UNLESS YOU TWO WANT ME TO SOFTEN HIM UP FOR YOU FIRST.
OH, YOU'LL SEE WHO DOES THE SOFTENING UP—
RAAARRR!
AAAHHHH!
MISTER TURTLE!
SCREEEEEEEEEEEEEECH

WHAT IS SHE DOING HERE?
AW, WHO'S YOUR FRIEND?
MISTER TURTLE'S BROTHERS!
CHLOE? YOU CAN'T BE HERE!
HAHAHAHA! HIDING BEHIND A CUB! JUST LIKE A COWARD.
OOH! YOU DIDN'T SAY YOU HAD A KITTY CAT!
OH NO! HE'S NOT A FRIENDLY CAT.
HA! IF YOU THINK A MERE CHILD CAN SAVE YOU, YOU ARE EVEN MORE PATHETIC WARRIORS THAN I THOUGHT.
HEY! I'LL SHOW YOU WHO'S A PATHETIC WARRIOR!
UM, RAPH, NOW MAY NOT BE THE TIME.
NO MORE MERCY!

RWAARR!
OOOOOH! TAG! YOU'RE IT, KITTY CAT MAN!
NOT NOW, CHLOE! JUST HANG ONTO ME.
I CAN'T BELIEVE YOU PICKED UP A LITTLE KID!
I TIRE OF THIS GAME! STOP RUNNING NOW AND I WILL LET THE CHILD GO BEFORE I SHELL YOU!
CAN WE DROP THAT KID OFF AND GET OUTTA HERE?!
IT'S NOT THAT SIMPLE, RAPH!
I DON'T KNOW. I ALWAYS WANTED A BABY SISTER. CAN WE KEEP HER?
MIKEY!
THE KID'S SLOWING US DOWN! WE SHOULD'VE TAKEN DOWN TIGER CLAW BY NOW!
IT'S NOT A RACE, RAPH!
COULDA FOOLED ME!

LEO, HOW ARE WE GONNA GET HER HOME?
EASIER SAID THAN DONE. I CAN SEE HER PLACE FROM HERE, BUT IT'S ON THE OTHER SIDE OF TIGER CLAW.
WHAT DO WE DO? GO THROUGH HIM?
COME OUT, COWARDS!
IF YOU HADN'T GONE OUT FOR TEA-TIME, WE WOULDN'T BE IN THIS MESS!
WELL, IF YOU WEREN'T CONSTANTLY BRAGGING, MAYBE WE WOULD HAVE SEEN WE WERE WALKING INTO A TRAP.
MISTER TURTLE'S BROTHERS! YOU SHOULD BE ASHAMED! CIVILIZED TURTLES GET ALONG.
YOU NEED TO COOL OFF!
OOH! LET'S GO SWIMMING IN THE FOUNTAIN? YOU'RE THE KIND OF TURTLES THAT LIKE WATER, RIGHT?
!
NOT REALLY, NO.
UM, WE CAN'T GO SWIMMING RIGHT NOW. WE'RE TRYING TO HIDE FROM THE GIANT TIGER MAN.
OH, WELL, CATS HATE GETTING WET.
THAT'S IT! THE FOUNTAIN! CHLOE, YOU'RE A GENIUS!
LISTEN UP, GUYS. SHE JUST GAVE ME AN IDEA.

YOU ARE MINE, REPTILES!
READY?
NOW!
TASTE SAI, TIGER CL-OW!
TAG! YOU'RE IT, MISTER TIGER!
CHLOE, STOP!
WRONG MOVE, CHILD!
SURRENDER TURTLES, OR I WILL TAKE THIS CUB AND—
GOTCHA, KID!
HA!
WHAT?

BOOM
ROAR!
SPLAAASH
I'VE CAUGHT YOU NOW!
CATCH THIS!
NO!
KCHING
AW YEAH! TIGER CLAW ON ICE!
MY FAVORITE SHOW.
BAD KITTY!
YEAH, DON'T MESS WITH THE TURTLE BROTHERS!
BRRR... I WILL HAVE MY REVENGE ON YOU... BRRR... TURTLES...
THAT WAS A GREAT GAME!
WE COULDN'T HAVE WON WITHOUT YOU, KID.
COME ON, LET'S GET YOU HOME.

LATER... JUST IN TIME FOR BED...
CAN YOU COME BACK EVERY NIGHT, MISTER TURTLE'S BROTHERS?
YOU'RE CUTE, KID, BUT WE GOT BAD GUYS TO BEAT DOWN EVERY NIGHT.
RAPH! AHEM, WHAT HE MEANS IS, BEING A TURTLE IS A DEMANDING JOB.
YEAH, ALL THE PIZZA IN NEW YORK ISN'T GONNA EAT ITSELF.
UGH... I DON'T LIKE PIZZA.
GASP DON'T LIKE... PIZZA?! LEO, WE GOTTA COME BACK, MAKE HER SEE THE LIGHT!
CAN YOU AT LEAST MAKE IT FOR TEA-TIME? YOU ALL HAVE TO LEARN TO BE CIVILIZED AND GET ALONG.
WE'LL SEE. MAYBE SOMEDAY.
OH NO! YOU WON'T CATCH ME AROUND A DOILY.
SHE'S RIGHT, RAPH. YOU DO NEED TO WORK ON YOUR DECORUM. OR CAN'T YO HANDLE NOT BEING THE BEST AT SOMETHING?

QUIET PLEASE
AHH... THE LIFE OF A SCIENTIST!
WE SCIENTIFICALLY INCLINED ARE NEITHER A "GLASS-HALF-FULL" TYPE, NOR A "GLASS-HALF-EMPTY" TYPE.
WE KNOW IT'S COMPLETELY FULL—JUST SOME OF THE CONTENTS ARE IN A LIQUID STATE, AND THE OTHERS ARE IN A VAPOR STATE!
HA! HA! HA!

NOW THEN... IF I'VE ISOLATED THE POLYMER PROPERLY, THIS *SHOULD*...

HEY, DONNIE!
LITTLE BUSY HERE, LEO.

SORRY! IT'S JUST THAT I'M SUPPOSED TO BE DOING MY KATAS WITH SENSEI, AND I'VE LOST ONE OF MY SWORDS.
YOU LOST ONE OF YOUR SWORDS?
WHAT? DID YOU GET INTO A ROOFTOP FIGHT WITH THE FOOT CLAN WHILE I WASN'T LOOKING?

STICK TO YOUR CHEMISTRY JOKES. THOSE ARE ALMOST FUNNY.
AND I DIDN'T "LOSE IT" SO MUCH AS MIKEY "BORROWED" IT.
LUNCH

HE "BORROWED" A MAGNIFYING GLASS ONCE. I FOUND IT THREE MONTHS LATER, COVERED IN JAM AND PEPPERONI.
BUT ANYWAY--HE HASN'T BEEN IN HERE LATELY. AND SINCE I'M IN THE MIDDLE OF SOMETHING...?
UH-HUH.
LUNCH

FINE. IF YOU SEE IT, LET ME KNOW.
YUH-HUH-WHATEVER-YOU-SAY-BYE!

ALRIGHT, SO... DID I NEED A CATALYST FOR THIS NEXT STEP?

GAH! WHAT WAS—?

HEY THERE. I'M BORED. HOW 'BOUT YOU?
ARGH! RAPH?!

OUT!
OF COURSE! WHAT WAS I THINKING, COMING TO YOU FOR FUN?

H'OKAY... SO... CATALYST OR NO CATALYST...?

AND THIS, ICE CREAM KITTY, IS DONNIE'S LAB! YOU REMEMBER THIS PLACE, DON'CHA?

AND RIGHT HERE WAS WHERE YOU WERE BORN! I MEAN—MUTATED! SAME THING, BASICALLY!
LUNCH

MICHELANGELO.
ARE YOU GETTING MUTATED BIOMASS ALL OVER MY PRECISION INSTRUMENTS?

LET'S GET OUT OF HERE. WHEN HE STARTS USING BIG WORDS—LIKE MY NAME—YOU *KNOW* HE'S MAD!

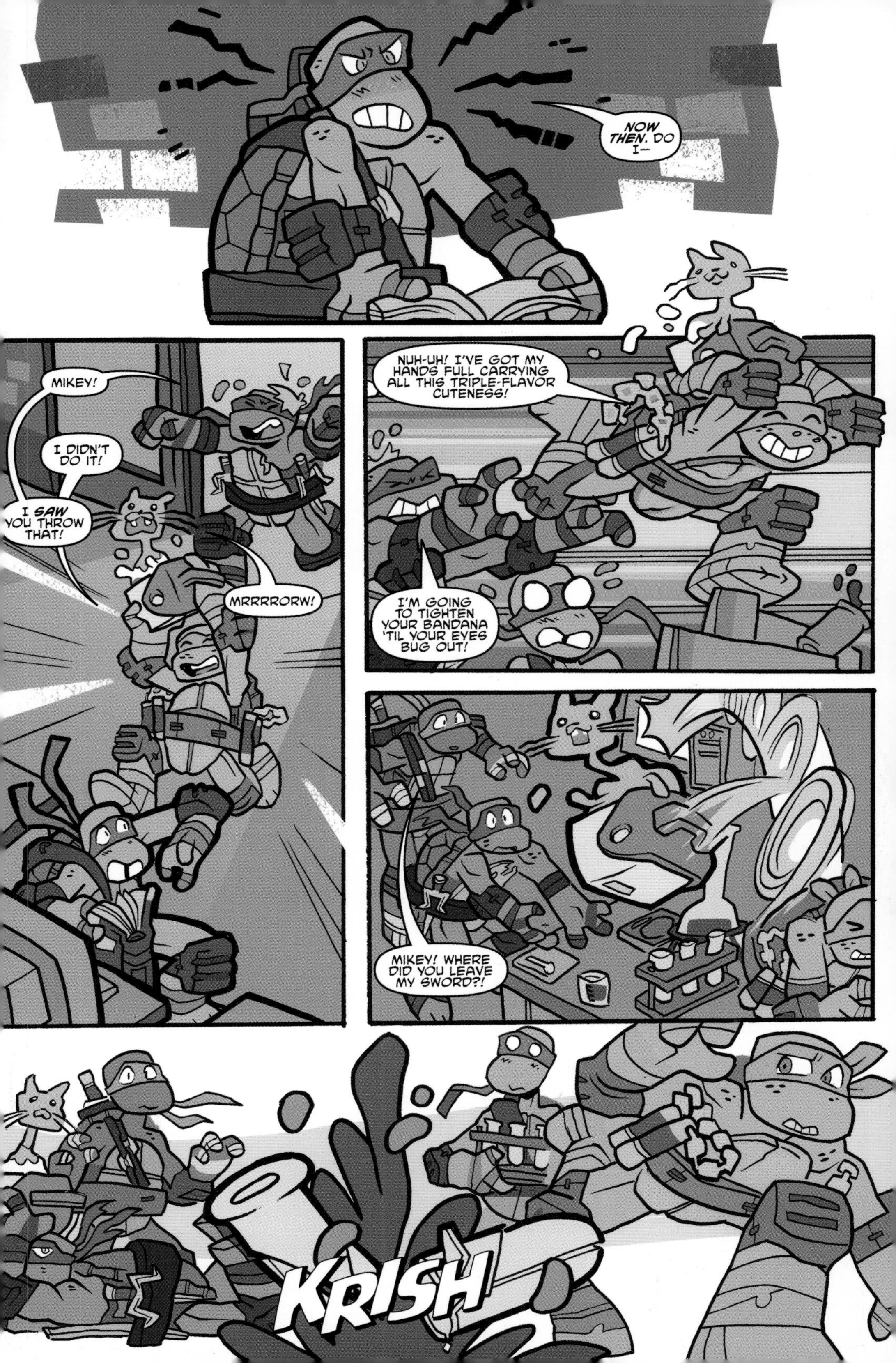
NOW THEN. DO I—
MIKEY!
I DIDN'T DO IT!
I SAW YOU THROW THAT!
MRRRRORW!
NUH-UH! I'VE GOT MY HANDS FULL CARRYING ALL THIS TRIPLE-FLAVOR CUTENESS!
I'M GOING TO TIGHTEN YOUR BANDANA 'TIL YOUR EYES BUG OUT!
MIKEY! WHERE DID YOU LEAVE MY SWORD?!
KRISH

THAT'S IT!
GET OUT! LEAVE! VACATE THE PREMISES! I. AM. TRYING. TO. WORK!
I DON'T DESERVE THIS. I SAVED THE CAT!
...BUT MY SWORD...?
OH! WAIT-WAIT-WAIT!
WHAT?
WE'RE STILL ON FOR THAT MARSHMALLOW AND BANANA PIZZA, RIGHT?
SLAM

AT LAST! PEACE AND QUIET!

YESSIR—THAT BLISSFUL SOUND OF NOTHING.

...IT'S TOO QUIET...

LATER...
BEEP
HONK
VROOOM

SCREEEEECH
KLIK
THERE YOU ARE! I'VE BEEN LOOKING ALL OVER FOR YOU.
HEY, APRIL!
WHAT ARE YOU DOING UP HERE?

AH, I JUST COULDN'T CONCENTRATE. I JUST NEEDED SOME WHITE NOISE TO WORK BY!
HONK
HOOOOOOOOOONK
WEE-OO
WEE-OO
CRASH

WE'RE HEADING OUT ON PATROL, SENSEI.
TIME TO POUND SOME BAD GUYS!
MY SONS, WAIT A MOMENT.
THE TOURNAMENT
I FEAR THE FOUR OF YOU ARE BECOMING TOO QUICK TO USE FORCE.
A TRUE NINJA MUST USE THEIR MIND FIRST. FIGHTING SHOULD ONLY BE SEEN AS THE LAST RESORT.
BUT IT'S ALSO THE FUNNEST RESORT.
HAI, SENSEI.
SEE? THERE'S SOMETHING TO BE SAID ABOUT BRAIN OVER BRAWN.
I'M SURE THERE IS BUT I DON'T WANT TO HEAR IT.
HMMFF.

DO YOU GUYS SMELL PIZZA?
I THINK YOU'RE EXPERIENCING WISHFUL SMELLING, MIKEY.
LOOKS LIKE WE MIGHT NOT FIND ANY TROUBLE TONIGHT, GUYS.
HEY, LEO?
LOOKS LIKE YOU SPOKE TOO SOON.
PURPLE DRAGONS!
ARCADE AND PIZZA
THIS IS OUR TURF, KID.
THAT MEANS EMPORIUM OWES US RENT.
UNHAND HIM, VILLAINS!
HAVE YOU EVER CONSIDERED NOT SAYING THINGS LIKE THAT?
EMPORIUM PIZZA & ARCADE
WAIT.
I'VE GOT AN IDEA.

HOW ABOUT A GAMING TOURNAMENT? TURTLES VERSUS DRAGONS. IF WE WIN, YOU HAVE TO LEAVE THIS PLACE ALONE FROM NOW ON.
?!
ARE YOU KIDDING ME?
REMEMBER WHAT MASTER SPLINTER SAID, RAPH. WE SHOULD STRIVE FOR VICTORY THROUGH THINKING INSTEAD OF POUNDING.
WHAT'S IN IT FOR US IF *WE* WIN?
YOU GET TO LEAVE WITH ALL OF YOUR TEETH?
HOW 'BOUT WHOEVER WINS GETS FREE PIZZA FOR A *YEAR?!*
A MONTH.
A MONTH!
DEAL.
THIS.
PLACE.
IS.
AWESOME!
WELCOME TO THE EMPORIUM!
BRAINS FOR LUNCH

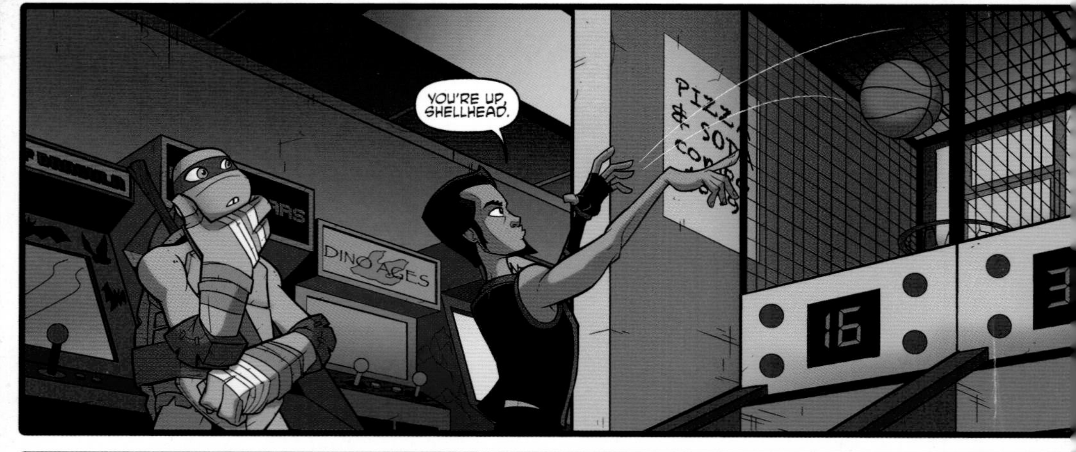
YOU'RE UP, SHELLHEAD.
DINO AGES
16

OK, DONATELLO—
—BRAIN OVER BRAWN.

OH, YEAH!

THAT'S RIGHT, BABY!

I DID IT!

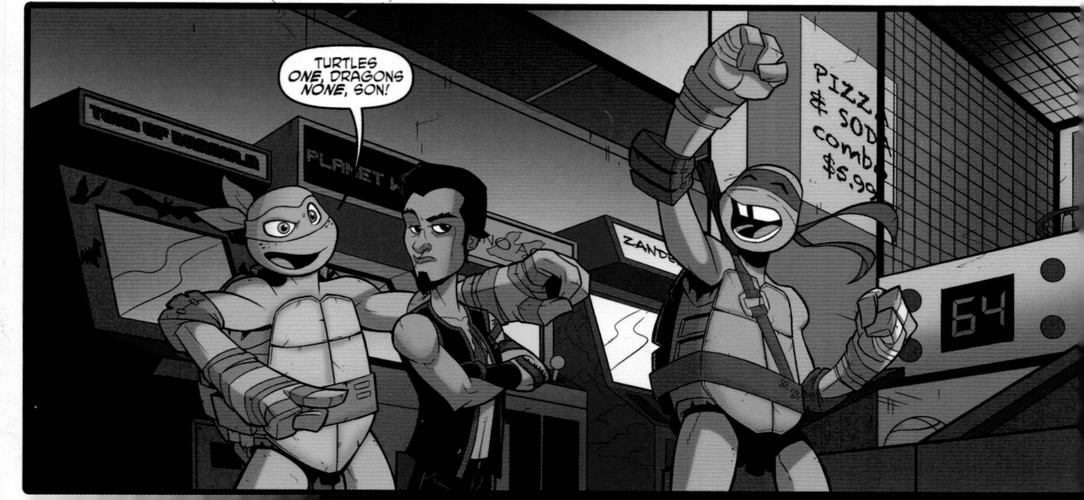
TURTLES *ONE*, DRAGONS *NONE*, SON!
64

SKEE 126 BALL
SKEE 000 BALL
SKEE 000 BALL
THIS LOOKS EASY ENOUGH.
YOU'RE GOIN' DOWN, PUNK.
WE'LL SEE, MUTANT.
AW, WHAT?!
TAKE YOUR TIME, RAPH.
BREATHE.
YEAH!
IN YOUR FACE, TURTLE.
OH, COME ON!
PERFECT SCORE!
THIS GAME IS IMPOSSIBLE!
DON'T SWEAT IT, MY NINJA.
I SHALL AVENGE YOU.
IT'S ALL IN THE WRIST, FREAK.
CALM DOWN, RAPH!
GRRRRRRR!

NEW HIGH SCORE!
ALL RIGHT!
DANCE MASTER
FOR A BIG GUY HE'S SURPRISINGLY FLEXIBLE.

YOU CALL *THAT* DANCING?
LEMME SHOW YOU HOW IT'S DONE, HOMIE.

AW YEAH, SON!

PLAYER 1
PERFECT!
SUPER COMBO!
I GOT THEM NINJA MOVES, Y'ALL!
NEW HIGH SCORE!
EXPERT
9272614028381

HE'S ALREADY BEAT YOUR SCORE AND HE'S NOT EVEN LOOKIN' AT THE SCREEN!
LIKE A TURTLE DO!

BOOYAKASHA!

ALL RIGHT. IN ORDER FOR THE DRAGONS TO STAY IN THE TOURNAMENT THEY HAVE TO WIN THIS NEXT GAME.
THE NEXT CHALLENGE IS—
—SPACE HEROES PINBALL!
I GOT THIS ONE, GUYS.
ARCADE
AND SO—
YOU WERE WORTHY OPPONENTS, PURPLE DRAGONS, BUT VICTORY IS OURS.
YEAH, WHATEVER.
THANKS, GUYS.
A DEAL'S A DEAL, FREE PIZZA FOR A MONTH.
"FREE" AND "PIZZA" ARE TOTALLY MY TWO FAVORITE WORDS!

TURTLE-POWER!
I AM PROUD OF YOU, MY SONS.
BY CHALLENGING THE PURPLE DRAGONS TO A CONTEST OF GAMING SKILLS, YOU HAVE SHOWN ME THAT YOU ARE ALL ON THE ROAD TO MATURITY—
THAT EMPORIUM PLACE SOUNDS COOL. MAYBE WE CAN GO THERE ON A DATE, RED?
MAYBE NOT, JONES.
HA!
EMPORIUM PIZZA
HEY, WHO ATE THE LAST SLICE AND DIDN'T THROW THE BOX AWAY?
—BUT THERE IS STILL WORK TO DO.

JOB SECURITY

OH, BOY... OH, NO...!
HA-HA!
WHUD
GRRR— I HAD HIM!
MIKEY! TURTLE WRECKING BALL!
NYET! I WAS HAVING HIM!
WOO! PIZZA GYOZA!
WHAM
"PIZZA GYOZA?" WHAT?
HEH HEH— SORRY. I MEANT TO SAY "BOOYAKASHA." I'M PRETTY HUNGRY.

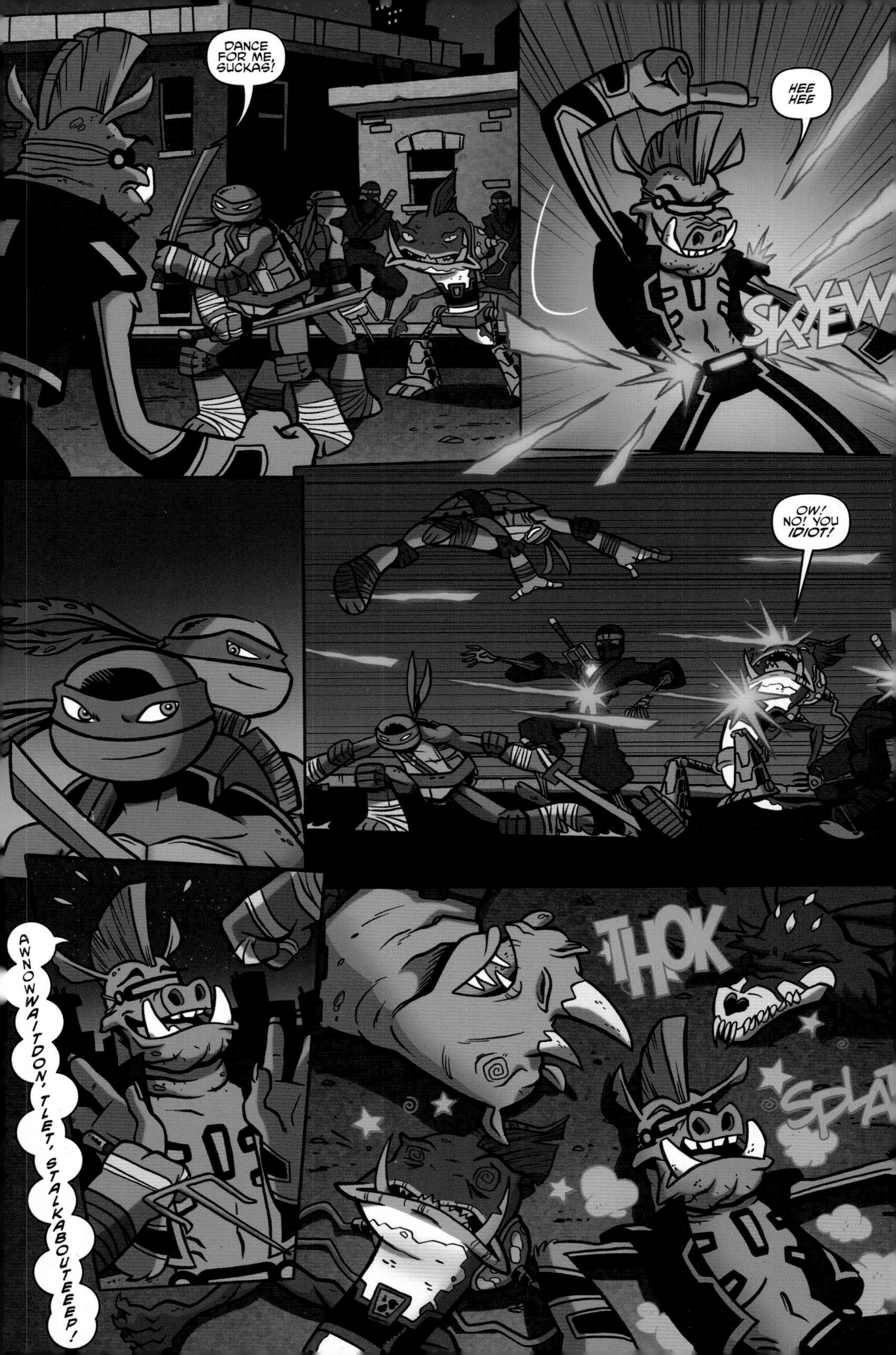
DANCE FOR ME, SUCKAS!
HEE HEE
SKYEW
OW! NO! YOU IDIOT!
AWNOWAITDON'TLET'STALKABOUTEEEP!
THOK
SPLAT

WELL... NO. WE CLIMBED BACK TO THE ROOF.
BUT BY THE TIME WE GOT BACK UP THERE, THE TURTLES HAD LEFT.
AND... UM... DESTROYED ALL THE... FOOT ROBOTS...
AND THEN YOU RETREATED?!
HOW UTTERLY PATHETIC.
EACH OF YOU WERE DANGEROUS MEN BEFORE YOU WERE MUTATED.
NOW, EVEN WITH YOUR ENHANCEMENTS AND MY ARMY, YOU CAN'T MANAGE AGAINST FOUR TEENAGERS.
IF YOU CANNOT CARRY YOUR WEIGHT IN MY ORGANIZATION, THEN YOU ARE DEAD WEIGHT. AND DEAD WEIGHT WILL BE PURGED.
PROVE YOUR VALUE BEFORE I DECIDE YOU'RE WORTHLESS.
HEY, FISHFACE. COME HERE A SECOND.

DON'T CALL ME THAT! MY NAME IS "XEVER!"
NO, "XEVER" DIDN'T HAVE GILLS.
YOU ARE FISHFACE—THE SLIMY MUTANT SERVING SHREDDER.
YOU WOULDN'T BE SAYING THAT IF EVERYONE STILL CALLED YOU "DOG POUND."
IT'S NOT FAIR YOU GOT A COOLER NAME WHEN YOU DOUBLE-MUTATED...
TAKE IT UP WITH MICHELANGELO. THAT'S NOT WHY I CALLED YOU OVER HERE.
"MASTER SHREDDER'S RIGHT. I USED TO BE HIS PROTEGE AND HEAD OF THE FOOT CLAN IN NEW YORK. YOU USED TO BE THE TERROR OF THE SOUTH AMERICAN UNDERWORLD. WE USED BE FEARED— RESPECTED.
"NOW WE'RE NO BETTER THAN THOSE GOONS ROCKSTEADY AND BEBOP."
I'VE NEVER LIKED YOU, BUT I LIKE DYING EVEN LESS.
WHAT DO YOU SAY? WE WORK TOGETHER TO REMIND MASTER SHREDDER WHAT WE'RE CAPABLE OF AND GET THOSE TWO "RETIRED?"
THE FEELING IS MUTUAL. LET'S DO IT— PARTNER.

HEY! YO! HOLD UP!
WHAT IS IT, BEBOP? I AM IN NO MOOD FOR YOUR NONSENSE.
OKAY— ONE? I HATE THAT NAME! QUIT USIN' IT!
WELL, I AM NOT BEING THE "ROCKSTEADY" ON MY OWN, SO BE GETTING USED TO IT.
AND TWO— IT WASN'T MY "NONSENSE" THAT MADE US PART OF SHREDDER'S FREAK SHOW!
"NYET... WE WERE HAVING GOOD DEAL UNTIL TURTLES SHOW UP.
"AND THEN RAHZAR AND FISHFACE DELIVERED US TO VERY CRANKY SHREDDER..."
YEAH, AND MY SUPER-SNIFFY PIG SNOUT IS SMELLIN' ANOTHER DOUBLE-CROSS BREWIN' BETWEEN MR. SKELETON PUPPY AND THE WALKIN'-TALKIN' SUSHI PLATTER.
THEN I WILL BREAK THEM...
AND TICK SHREDDER OFF WITH IN-FIGHTING?
I KNOW YOU LIKE THE DIRECT APPROACH, BUT TRUST ME—WE GOTTA STEAL THIS VICTORY FROM THEM.
LISTEN UP—I GOT A PLAN...

I AM NOT UNDERSTANDING. IF WE BLOW UP TURTLES AND DELIVER THEIR LITTLE BITS, HOW WILL SHREDDER KNOW IT WAS THEM?
RAHZAR AND FISHFACE WILL BE SAYING IT'S JUST CAN OF HASH WE USE AS TRICK.
'CAUSE *THESE* LITTLE BABIES ARE TECH OF MY *OWN* DESIGN! THESE *"DUB-STOMP" MINES* PACK ALL THE WALLOP OF THEIR EXPLOSIVE COUSINS, BUT THEY'RE NON-LEATHAL.
I AIN'T CUTTIN' THEM TURTLES BOYS *NO* SLACK, THO'! THEY'LL BE TOO WEAK TO PUT UP A FIGHT!
HAHAHA! ONCE THE FOOT-BOTS LURE TURTLES HERE, THEY CHARGE US, SET OFF MINES—
AND *BLAMMO!*
"BEST OF ALL—WE'LL MAKE BRADFORD AND XEVER LOOK LIKE CHUMPS!"
"YOU ARE MEANING RAHZAR AND—"
"I KNOW WHAT I SAID!"

SO... THE TURTLES DESTROY OUR FOOT-BOT DECOYS. THEY COME IN TO FIND US AND... KINDLY GET INTO THE TRAPS FOR US?
THESE THINGS HAVE HELD THEM BEFORE. ONCE WE AMBUSH THEM, THEY'LL BE TOO BUSY FIGHTING FOR THEIR LIVES TO WATCH THEIR FOOTING.

I DON'T KNOW...
YOU GOT A BETTER IDEA? I HAVEN'T SEEN YOU USE THOSE POISON FANGS OF YOURS LATELY!
HAVE *YOU* TASTED THEM? THEY LIVE IN THE *SEWER!*

ALL RIGHT! ALL SET! WE'LL HIDE IN THE ALLEY SO WE'RE NOT—

WHAT-THE-*WHA?!*
—SPOTTED?!

OH! *AHEH-HEH... BOA NOITE.* WHAT... *AH...* BRINGS YOU TWO OUT HERE?

WE... ARE... DUMPSTER-DIVING! DA, THAT'S IT!
YOU WOULDN'T ***BELIEVE*** WHAT SOME PEOPLE PUT IN THE TRASH!

WHAT'S "GARBAGE" IS YOUR EXCUSES! YOU'RE OUT HERE TRYING TO ONE-UP US AND CAPTURE THE TURTLES!

LOOKS LIKE THE CAT'S OUTTA THE BAG, OL' BUDDY.
DA...

...AND THE WARTHOG IS OUT OF THE DUMPSTER!
HEE-HEE
CLONK
FORGET IMPRESSING THE BOSS! LET'S JUST GIVE HIM TEN POUNDS OF IVORY!
I WILL FIND WAY TO STUFF YOU INTO SINGLE TUNA CAN!
WMMM
BOOM

SEE? I TOLJA THOSE FOOT BOTS WERE ACTING SUSPICIOUS!
WHAT CAN I SAY, MIKEY? YOU WERE RIGHT AFTER ALL.
OOH-OOH! WHAT DO I WIN?
FOUR OF SHREDDER'S GOONS TO WHUP TO YOUR HEART'S DELIGHT!
GET 'EM!
BOO-YAKASHAAA!
BEEP
WAIT!
BWOOOOOOOOOOOOMP

ARRRGH... IDIOT! YOU COULD'VE MADE US ALL DEAF!
WHAT?
I SAID--!
--NEVERMIND...
...WE JUST CAPTURED THE TURTLES!

THE FOOT MUTANTS ARE IN COMPETITION TO CAPTURE THE TURTLES. DESPITE THEIR EFFORTS TO ONE-UP EACH OTHER, THEIR COMBINED EFFORTS HAVE CAUSED THEM TO ACCIDENTALLY SUCCEED!
YES! WE DID IT! WE *FINALLY* DID IT!

VICTORY IS OURS!

...AT WHAT POINT DID WE LOSE CONTROL OF THE SITUATION HERE?

STAY CALM, GUYS. WE'LL GET THROUGH THIS.
SOMEHOW.
HAHAHA! TINY TURTLES FELL FOR OUR CUNNING TRAPS!

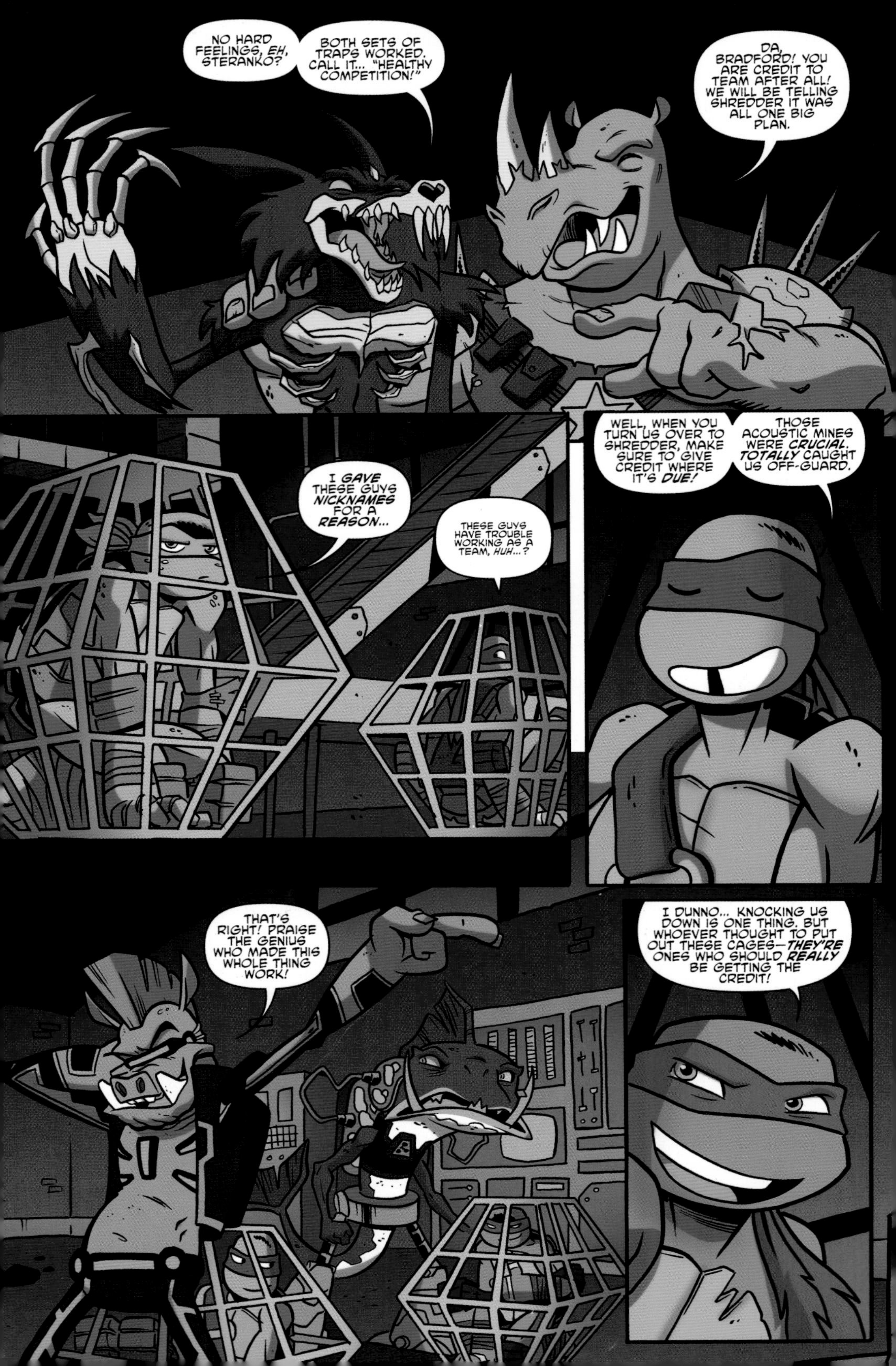
NO HARD FEELINGS, EH, STERANKO?
BOTH SETS OF TRAPS WORKED. CALL IT... "HEALTHY COMPETITION!"
DA, BRADFORD! YOU ARE CREDIT TO TEAM AFTER ALL! WE WILL BE TELLING SHREDDER IT WAS ALL ONE BIG PLAN.
I GAVE THESE GUYS NICKNAMES FOR A REASON...
THESE GUYS HAVE TROUBLE WORKING AS A TEAM, HUH...?
WELL, WHEN YOU TURN US OVER TO SHREDDER, MAKE SURE TO GIVE CREDIT WHERE IT'S DUE!
THOSE ACOUSTIC MINES WERE CRUCIAL. TOTALLY CAUGHT US OFF-GUARD.
THAT'S RIGHT! PRAISE THE GENIUS WHO MADE THIS WHOLE THING WORK!
I DUNNO... KNOCKING US DOWN IS ONE THING. BUT WHOEVER THOUGHT TO PUT OUT THESE CAGES—THEY'RE ONES WHO SHOULD REALLY BE GETTING THE CREDIT!

HE'S RIGHT. AND YOU DOUBTED ME.
YES, YES. WE WON, ALL THANKS TO YOU. IT'S JUST WE'VE DONE THE "HORDE OF FOOTBOTS" THING SO MANY TIMES...
NYET! FOOTBOT DECOYS WERE OUR PLAN!
AND YOU WOULDN'T HAVE CAUGHT A COLD, MUCH LESS THOSE TURTLES, IF MY MINES HADN'T TAKEN 'EM DOWN FIRST!
NO--WE SENT FOOT BOTS TO LURE THE TURTLES!
WHAT A "SURPRISE." THE MASTER THIEF AND ARMS SMUGGLER ARE OUT TO STEAL OUR VICTORY!
NO! NO! NO! I AM NOT GETTING POPPED EARDRUMS JUST FOR YOU TWO TO STEAL THE GLORY!
WHAT'S THAT, COMRADE? CRUSH THEM BOTH? GOOD IDEA.
...DIDN'T THEY BOTH SEND OUT FOOT BOTS?
MIKEY! SHH!
AAAAAAAAAAAAAHHHHHHHHHHHH

I BET YOU A PIZZA I CAN MAKE THIS WORSE. AND BY "WORSE" I MEAN "BETTER."
YOU'RE ON!
WHAT ARE YOU DOING?!
HUH?
YOU'VE GOT AN ARSENAL HIDDEN IN YOUR OUTFIT! DON'T TAKE HIM HEAD-ON! USE ALL YOUR AWESOME GEAR!
HEY NOW! WHEN YOU'RE RIGHT—YOU'RE RIGHT!
ARGH!
RARGH!
EEE-HEE!

SOK
CLANG
I SEE YOUR PIZZA, DON, AND RAISE YOU AN EXTRA LARGE!
YOU CAN DO BETTER THAN THAT, FISHFACE! I KNOW--WE'VE FOUGHT TO A STAND-STILL!
QUIT USING YOUR FLIMSY ARMS AND PUT THOSE ROBO-LEGS TO WORK!
THWAK

PIZZA?! I WANT IN ON THIS!
COME ON, RAHZAR! YOU CAN'T LET THE NEW GUY WIN!
YOU'RE PERSONALLY TRAINED BY SHREDDER! YOU'VE HAD TWO NICKNAMES!
YOU'RE WAY MORE EVIL-ER THAN HIM!
GO GIVE HIM A DOG-POUNDING, RAHZAR!
RAAAARGH!
AHH! AHHHH! WAITAMINUTELET'STALKTHIS—
AHHHHH!

I DON'T KNOW IF TAKING BETS RIGHT NOW IS THE BEST...
HUH?
OH! UH...
WELL?
IT IS YOUR TURN TO BE GIVING PEP-TALK!
YOU... FIGHT WITH TWO WEAPONS! I DO TOO!
AND THAT EXPERIENCE HAS TAUGHT ME THAT TWO IS BETTER THAN ONE!
THIS WILL DO!
RAAAAUGH!
VMP
I WILL MAKE FISH-STICK OUT OF YOU!
YOU'RE AS WEAK AS YOUR FISH PUNS!

STAY!
C'MON, ROBOT-LEGS! LET'S KICK IT!
COME ON, PORCO! GIVE ME YOUR BEST SHOT!

HEH HEH... TAKE *THAT*, YOU...
WHAT WAS...?
...XEVER...?
...BEBOP...?

...SMOKE GRENADE?!
BWOOSH
SCREEEEEECH

AW MAN! THEY GOT AWAY!
SO... WHO WON THE PIZZA FROM WHO AGAIN?
WE ALL WON. YOUR TREAT.
"TWO IS BETTER THAN ONE?" YOU'LL FORGIVE ME IF I FIND YOUR ASSESSMENT A LITTLE SPECIOUS.
UH-HUH. AND HOW MANY BO STAFFS HAVE YOU GONE THROUGH?

I CERTAINLY WASN'T EXPECTING A LAST-MINUTE RESCUE FROM YOU...

...TIGER CLAW.
I SAW THE FOUR OF YOU ALL CONSPIRING AGAINST EACH OTHER.
I KNEW YOU WOULD DO SOMETHING STUPID, SO I FOLLOWED YOU AND PREPARED FOR THE WORST.

WELL— THAT'S IT! ONCE YOU TATTLE ON US, HE'S GONNA END US ALL!
I AM NOT GOING TO... "TATTLE."

WE ARE ALL IN SERVICE TO THE SHREDDER NOW.
WE HAVE NO AMBITIONS OF OUR OWN, SAVE TO SERVE HIS WILL.
AS YOUR FELLOW SOLDIER—AS A FELLOW MUTANT—I WILL KEEP TONIGHT A SECRET.
LET IT BE A LESSON FOR YOU ALL.
WELL... I THINK IT'S CLEAR WE ALL HATE EACH OTHER...
DA.
ABSOLUTAMENTE!
YOU CAN SAY THAT AGAIN.
...BUT WE HATE THE TURTLES MORE! DEATH TO THE TURTLES!
DEATH TO THE TURTLES!

GOOD WORK, GUYS. I FEEL LIKE MASTER SPLINTER WAS PRETTY HAPPY WITH OUR TRAINING TODAY.
I CAN COUNT THE AMOUNT OF TIMES HE SCOLDED US ON JUST ONE 3-FINGERED HAND!
IF YOU ASK ME, WE NEEDED IT AFTER LAST NIGHT...
YOU WIN SOME, YOU SHOE SOME!
OH, I DON'T KNOW. LAST NIGHT WASN'T SO BAD...
MAYBE NOT FOR YOU!
WE'D JUST CHASED OFF THE FOOT FROM THAT CONSTRUCTION SITE ON NORFOLK WHEN POOR CASEY GOT CAUGHT IN SOME *CURING CONCRETE!*
BUT ALAS! OUR CRUSADING COMPADRE HAD TO CAST OFF HIS KICKS BEFORE HE COULD SHARE IN OUR VICTORY DANCE!
OH C'MON, IT COULD HAPPEN TO ANYONE... I MEAN, NOT US, BUT...
...A BIG CASEY JONES HELLO TO MY HALFSHELL-ED HOMBRES!

NOTICE ANYTHING DIFFERENT?
PING

UM... NEW HAIRCUT?
MUSTACHE COMING IN?
DIRTIER HOODIE?
LOSE ANOTHER TOOTH?

I GOT AWESOME NEW SHOES!

PRETTY RAD, RIGHT? MY IDEAL ALL-AROUND COMBAT KICKS.
SUCH ICONIC DESIGN!
A MINIMALIST DROP, WITH A STURDY NEAR-TACTICAL UPPER!
AND A TREAD THAT KEEPS YOUR FOOTING SURE AT ANY SPEED!
(TURNS OUT I KNOW A LOT ABOUT FOOTWEAR.)
SO WHY DON'T *WE* WEAR SHOES?

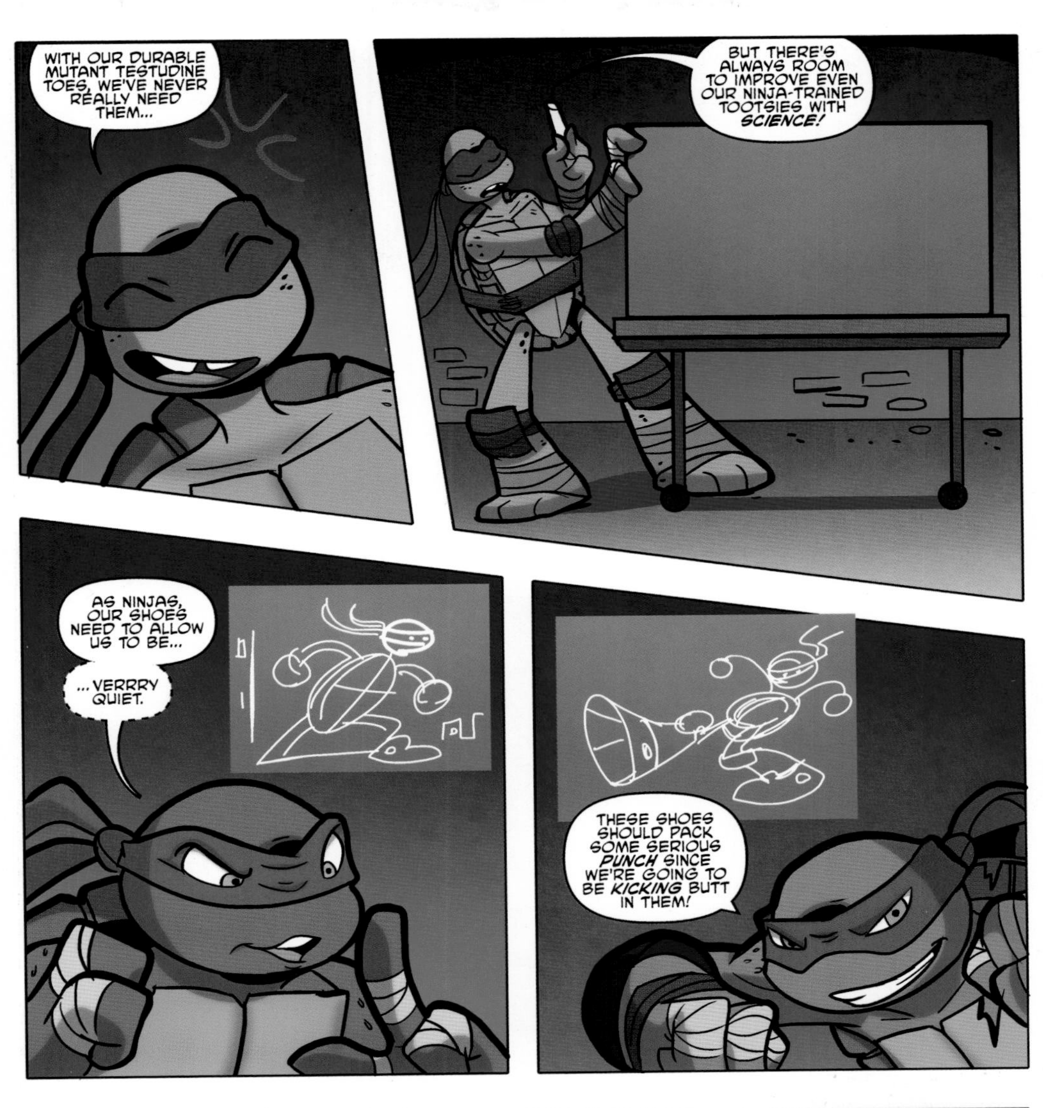
WITH OUR DURABLE MUTANT TESTUDINE TOES, WE'VE NEVER REALLY NEED THEM...
BUT THERE'S ALWAYS ROOM TO IMPROVE EVEN OUR NINJA-TRAINED TOOTSIES WITH *SCIENCE!*
AS NINJAS, OUR SHOES NEED TO ALLOW US TO BE...
...VERRRY QUIET.
THESE SHOES SHOULD PACK SOME SERIOUS *PUNCH* SINCE WE'RE GOING TO BE *KICKING* BUTT IN THEM!

WE GOTTA LOOK FRESH FOR SURE, FROM STREET TO SEWER.

AND LIKE ANY 21ST CENTURY WEARABLE, IT SHOULD INCLUDE THE LATEST SMART FEATURES!
TIME TO GET TO WORK!

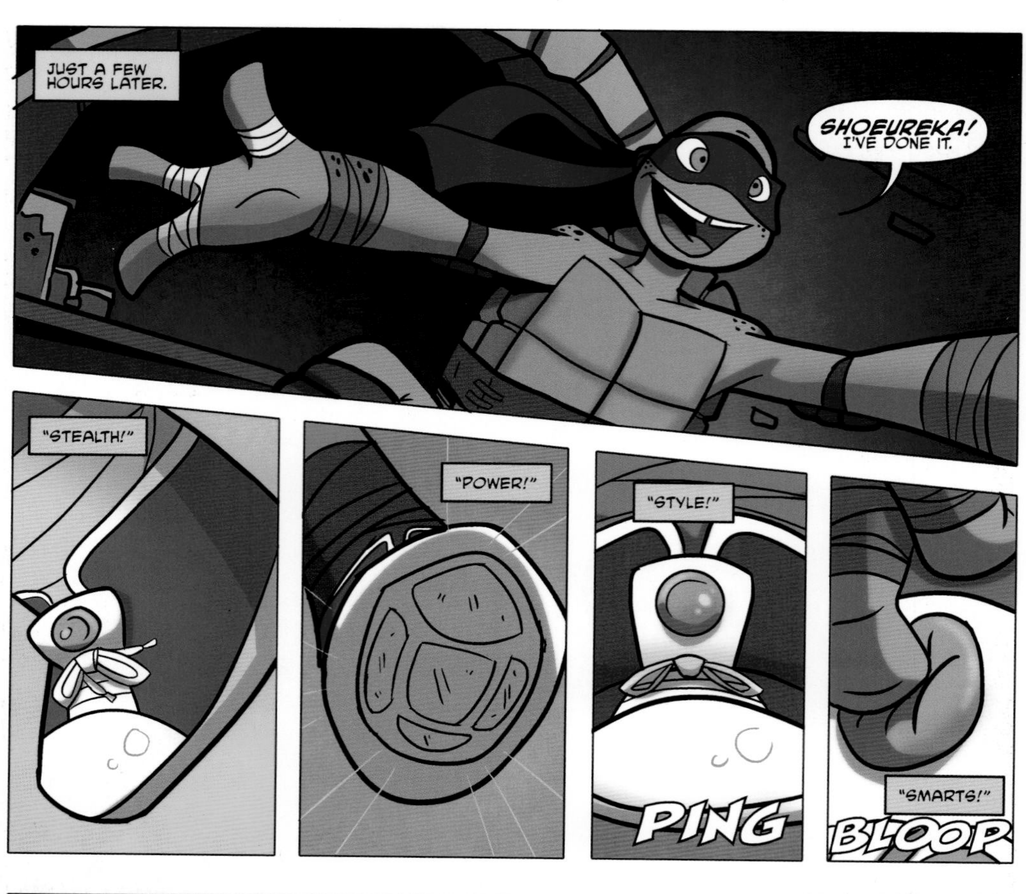
JUST A FEW HOURS LATER.
SHOEUREKA! I'VE DONE IT.
"STEALTH!"
"POWER!"
"STYLE!"
PING
"SMARTS!"
BLOOP

"SUH-WEET! NOW LET'S HIT THE STREETS."
WELL, THAT DIDN'T TAKE LONG.
THOSE PUNKS ARE BITING OUR STYLE!
TIME TO SEE WHAT DONNIE'S NEW SHOES CAN DO.

CAREFUL WITH THESE, PURPLE DRAGONS.
THE TINIEST OF SCUFFS DISRESPECT NOT ONLY *YOUR FEET*, BUT ALSO *THE FOOT*.
GET YOUR *HANDS* OFF THOSE, CREEPS!
THE TURTLES!
LEAVE THE *SHOES*, HUN, OR YOU'RE GONNA GET *SOCKED*.
WOOOAH!
KWICK
URK!
WHOK
I DON'T KNOW WHY YOU DWEEBS STEP UP. WE ALWAYS BEAT YOU.
HUH. MAYBE DONNIE MADE THESE SOLES *TOO* POWERFUL?
SO EASILY DISTRACTED!
OOF!

HERE I COME, STRUTTIN' MY STUFF IN MY NEW DANCIN' SHOES!
KWAK
GRAAA!
AW MAAAN! MY PRISTINE SNEAKS ARE ALREADY SHOWING THEIR 20-MINUTE AGE! A LITTLE WIPE SHOULD DO THE TRI—

WAOOH! TAKE THAT, HIGH FASHION TOURIST!

END THIS QUICKLY, PURPLE DRAGONS!

EH?!
TSK. RUBBER SOLES...
SQUEAK!

CONSIDER THIS DIVINE PUNISHMENT FOR BEING SHOE NOOBS!
WHAM
GWAH!

IT SEEMS ONE OF YOU FOOLS IS STILL STANDING.
C'MON, GUYS. YOU MAY BE NEW TO SHOES, BUT YOU AIN'T NEW TO FIGHTING! LET'S DO THIS!
NINJAS. LET'S *SHOE* HUN WHO HE'S DEALING WITH.
I AM SO JEALOUS I DIDN'T SAY THAT!
WHAT? YOU DISGRACE YOUR FOOTWEAR SO PLAINLY?
BOMP
OOF!
SHOE TALK TOO MUCH!
HURK!
ALL THE GOOD JOKES ARE TAKEN! JUST FALL OVER!
WHOP

HURK THAT'S RIGHT. RUN, TURTLES.
SUCH PITIFUL RESTRAINTS CANNOT HOLD THE MIGHT OF THE PURPLE DRAGONS...
...FOR *GRRK* MUCH LONGER, THAT IS... 10 MINUTES, TOPS!
SORRY GUYS, I GOT SO CAUGHT UP IMPLEMENTING COOL SHOE FEATURES THAT I DIDN'T PROPERLY CALCULATE THE SUM OF THEIR PARTS.
I GUESS FOR US, OUR PLAIN 'OL FEET ARE THE BEST ALL-AROUND FOOTWEAR?
SORRY WE GAVE YOU A HARD TIME ABOUT LOSING YOUR OLD SHOES IN THE FIGHT YESTERDAY, CASEY.
LIKE ANY NINJA GEAR, I GUESS THEY REQUIRE SOME TRAINING TO BE EFFECTIVE.
ARE YOU KIDDING ME? TONIGHT WAS AWESOME.
THAT'S EXACTLY WHAT YOU'RE SUPPOSED TO DO WITH NEW SHOES!
TAKE IT FROM CASEY JONES. SHOES ARE MEANT TO BE BROKEN IN AND WORN OUT!

"COWA-BOOYAKASHA"

BOOYAKASHA!

PFFFT!
COWA-BUNGA.
BOO.
YAKA.
SHA.

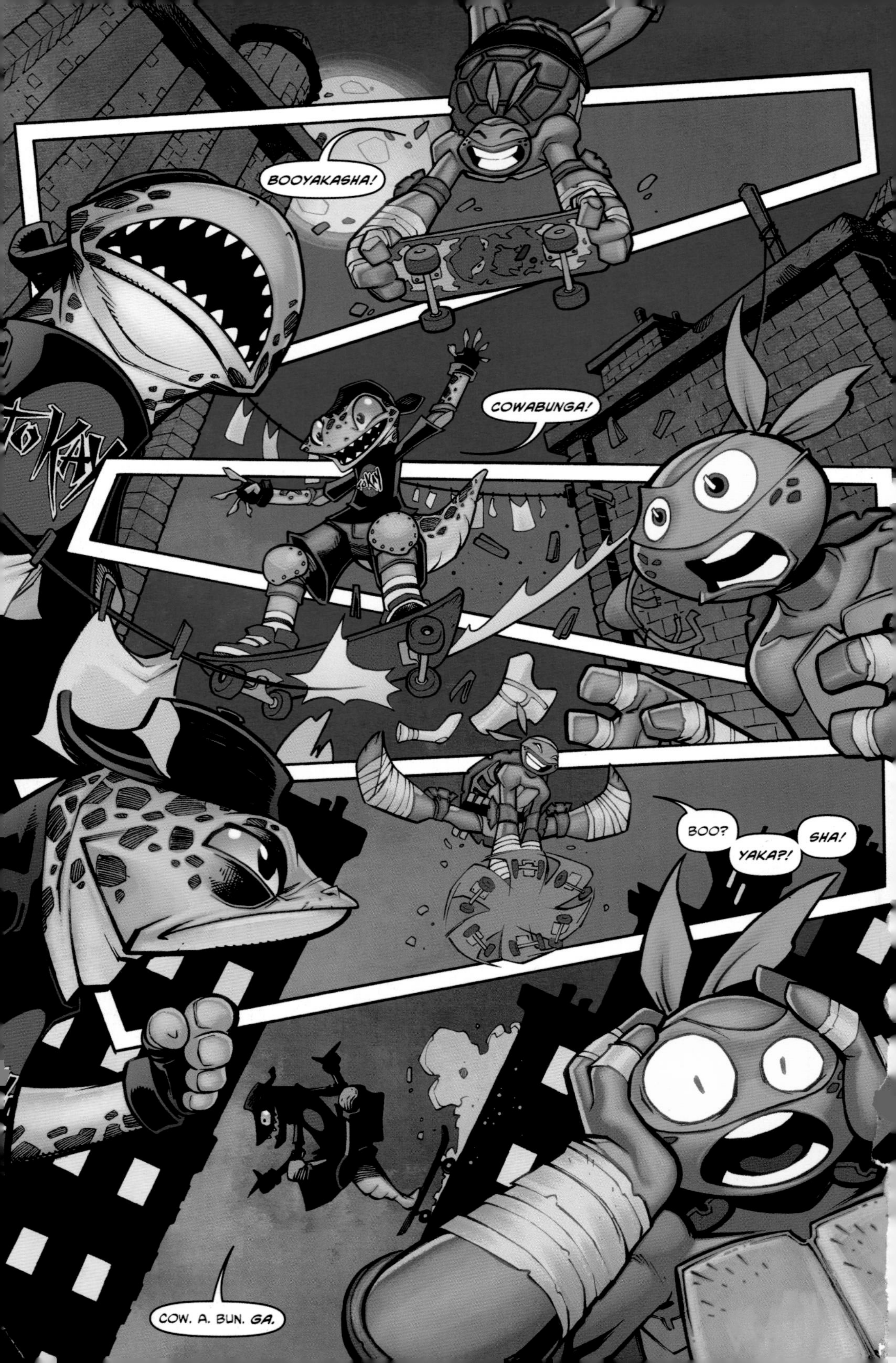
BOOYAKASHA!
COWABUNGA!
BOO?
YAKA?!
SHA!
COW. A. BUN. GA.

BOO!
COW!
A!
YA!
KA!
BUN!
SHA!
GA!
COW-A-BUN--GA?!
BOO. BOO-YAKA SHA.
COWA! OWA! BUNGA!
BOO-OO. YA-YA. KA-KA. SHA-SHA.

...COWABUNGA...
BOO. YAKASHA.
COWA... GULP... BUNGA?
BOO-YAKASHA!
CLAP!

COWA-
BOON-
KASHA!

COWABUNGA?
BOOYAKASHA.